Molly Mischief

Saves the World!

First published in the United Kingdom in 2018 by
Pavilion Children's Books
43 Great Ormond Street
London
WC1N 3HZ

An imprint of Pavilion Books Limited

Publisher and Editor: Neil Dunnicliffe
Art Director and Designer: Lee-May Lim

ISBN: 9781843653585

A CIP catalogue record for this book is available from the British Library

10 9 8 7 6 5 4 3 2 1

Reproduction by Mission, Hong Kong
Printed by Toppan Leefung Printing Ltd, China

This book can be ordered directly from the publisher online
at www.pavilionbooks.com, or try your local bookshop.

Molly Mischief

Saves the World!

Adam Hargreaves

PAVILION

Hello, my name is Molly.
Most of the time I'm happy – happy making mischief.

That's why I'm called Molly Mischief!

But some things make me unhappy. Things like chores.

I don't like tidying my room.
But when I *do* tidy my room, Mum's not happy!

There's no pleasing her.

I don't like unpacking
the groceries.
But when I *do* unpack the
groceries, Dad's not happy.
There's no pleasing him!
Food
Food
Fruit Gloops
MOLLY!

And I don't like washing up.
But when I *do* the washing up, my brother's not happy.

Sometimes there's no pleasing anyone!

I wish I could do all my chores in supersonic time.
I wish I had superpowers.
I wish I could be a superhero.

So I went upstairs and got dressed as...

SUPER-MOLLY!

I tidied my bedroom in super-quick time.

I vacuumed,
SUPER-MOLLY!
and polished,
SUPER-MOLLY!

put away the dishes,

SUPER-MOLLY!

mopped, **SUPER-MOLLY!**

and took out the rubbish. ALL in the blink of an eye!

I had *lots* of superpowers.
I was very **STRONG.**
I had **LASER EYES.**

I could walk on the ceiling.
Woof!
Woof!
Woof!
Woof!
Woof!
I could talk to animals.
I could leap over
TALL
buildings in
a single bound!

And I could fly!

Up! Up! Up!

And away!

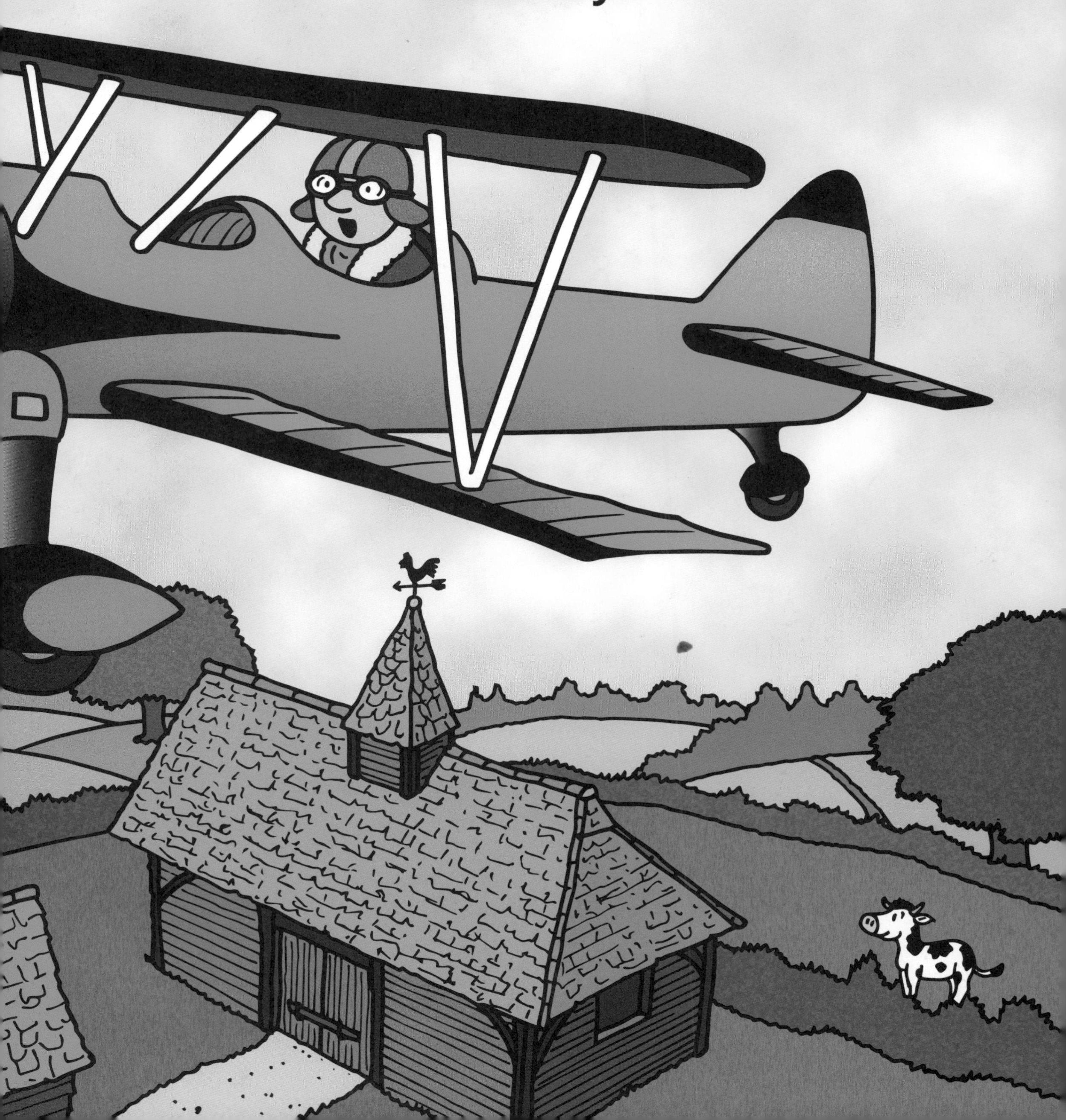

I discovered I could drink
15 milkshakes in 15 seconds!
Although I am not sure that
was such a good idea.

And you ought to have seen me on my bike!

It was great fun having lots of superpowers.

It was also very useful.
It was useful when the bully at school tried to take my lunch money.

And it was useful when we got stuck in a traffic jam.

I helped an old lady cross the road, at *super speed.*

And then I realised I could be a real-life superhero.

I saved a cow from a tornado.
MOO!

I rescued a **whale** at the seaside!

Sport
Super-Molly wins the Tour de Bike
Daily News
Super-Molly Saves Cow!

And I saved the world from a meteorite!

Super-Molly became super-famous.
She was on the front page of the paper and starred on the TV news.

But nobody knew it was me.
Nobody knew all the good deeds I was doing.
It's no fun being famous and not being recognised.
It's no fun being good and not getting praise.

Being a superhero was also hard work.
I had to get up in the middle of the night to fight crime.

I had to miss my favourite dinner to capture an escaped lion.

And cleaning up the flood was no fun at all.

In fact, being a superhero was just one long list of chores!

So, I gave up being Super-Molly.

I decided it was much easier to do what I'm told.
Well, most of the time.

I *have* kept one superpower.
One superpower I would never give up.
I am super...

...Mischievous!